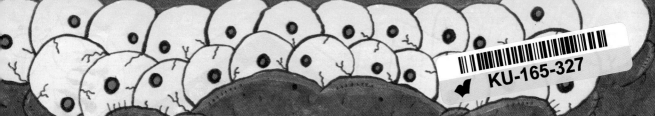

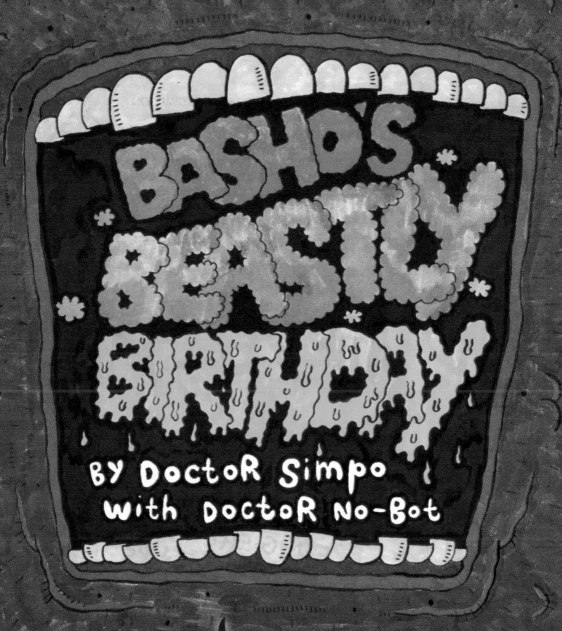

BASHO'S BEASTLY BIRTHDAY

BY DOCTOR SIMPO
WITH DOCTOR NO-BOT

PIQUANT
editions

BASHO'S MUMS HOUSE.
KEEP OFF YOU DIRTY
FINGERED ROBBER
TYPES!
BASHO'd '08

WHEN THE BOYS AND GIRLS OPEN THEIR INVITATIONS THEY ARE PLEASED TO FIND THAT BASHO'S PARTY WILL BE A FANCY-DRESS BEASTLY BIRTHDAY BONANZA!!!

MEANWHILE:

MARGO BUILDS A QUAD-WINGED, QUAD-HEADED
LEO DOMINI COSTUME WITH LOTS OF SPOTS!

FITZ RIGS UP A BEAR RIB-THROAT EAT-EM-UP SUIT COMPLETE WITH A BEAST-ROAR VOICE MANIPULATOR!

BASHO PLAYS WITH HIS NEW TOYS FOR ALL OF 5
MINUTES AND THEN SUDDENLY STOPS. SHEER BOREDOM
SETS IN. HE'S GOT WHAT HE WANTED AND YET HE
DOESN'T SEEM TO FEEL HAPPY. "YEAH WHATEVER..."
HE SAYS, PUSHING ASIDE WALKING-TALKING ROBOTS,
A MEGAZONE 1,000,000 GAMES-CONSOLE UNIT WITH
BUILT IN VIRTUAL-REALITY BATTLE-BEAST ZONE AND
THE GREEN MUTANT FLYING FROG-FISH.
WHAT DOES HE REALLY WANT?

THEN A VERY ORDINARY THING HAPPENS. A LETTER
DROPS THROUGH THE MAIL SLOT. HE NOTICES THAT
THE NEIGHBOUR'S DOG MUST HAVE BEEN AT THE
POSTMAN AGAIN
JUDGING BY A WET
RING OF TEETH-
MARKS ON ONE END.
BUT BASHO
REMEMBERS THAT
THE POSTMAN HAD
ALREADY BEEN,
EARLIER THAT DAY.
BASHO IS ABOUT TO
FIND OUT THAT
EXTRAORDINARY
THINGS CAN COME
IN ORDINARY
PACKAGES...!

THE LETTER READS... DEAR BASHO BUTTERCREAM, FIRSTLY I WOULD LIKE TO CONGRATULATE YOU ON YOUR SPECIAL DAY. I HOPE THAT YOU GOT EVERYTHING THAT YOU WANTED. BUT MAYBE, JUST MAYBE, YOU GOT THE THINGS THAT YOU THOUGHT YOU WANTED AND THE THINGS THAT YOU THOUGHT WOULD MAKE YOU HAPPY. PERHAPS YOU STILL FEEL A LITTLE EMPTY INSIDE. PERHAPS YOU WOULD LIKE TO RECEIVE THE GREATEST GIFT OF ALL. HOWEVER, I WARN YOU NOW THAT IT WON'T BE EASY AND THERE WILL BE NO TURNING BACK ONCE YOU HAVE SET OFF ON YOUR ADVENTURE. BUT IF YOU THINK YOU ARE UP TO THE CHALLENGE, THEN TRY TO FOLLOW ME IF YOU CAN! SIGNED BY THE 'SEVEN-EYED SEVEN-HORNED LAMBMAN'. OUT OF THE CORNER OF SOME OF HIS EYES THE MYSTERIOUS SENDER LOOKS BACK THROUGH THE WINDOW AS BASHO LOOKS UP TO MEET HIS GAZE.

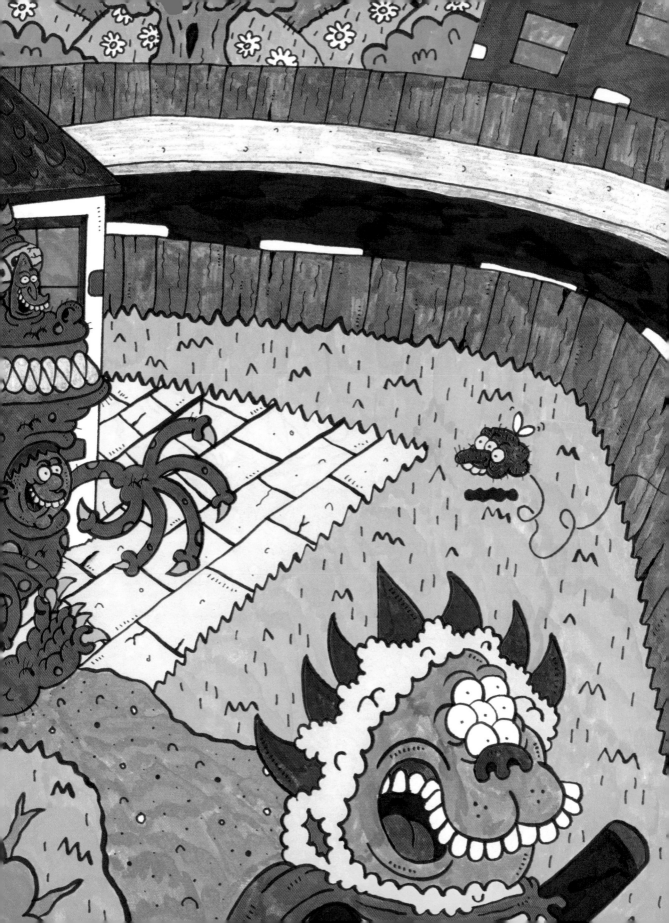

BASHO IS DETERMINED TO FOLLOW LAMBMAN AND
FIND OUT WHAT THIS IS ALL ABOUT — NO MATTER
WHAT! EVEN IF IT MEANS WADING THROUGH
A DUCK POND...

...EVEN IF IT MEANS RAMBLING THROUGH A ROCKERY...

...OR WALKING THROUGH A WOOD...

...OR HIKING UP A HILLOCK...

BASHO, EXHAUSTED, FINALL
SEVEN-EYED SEVEN-HORNE
SAYS LAMBMAN, "NOW THAT W
YOU A GREAT GIFT...IT WAS WRITTE
...HERE'S SIR RAPH, WHO WIL

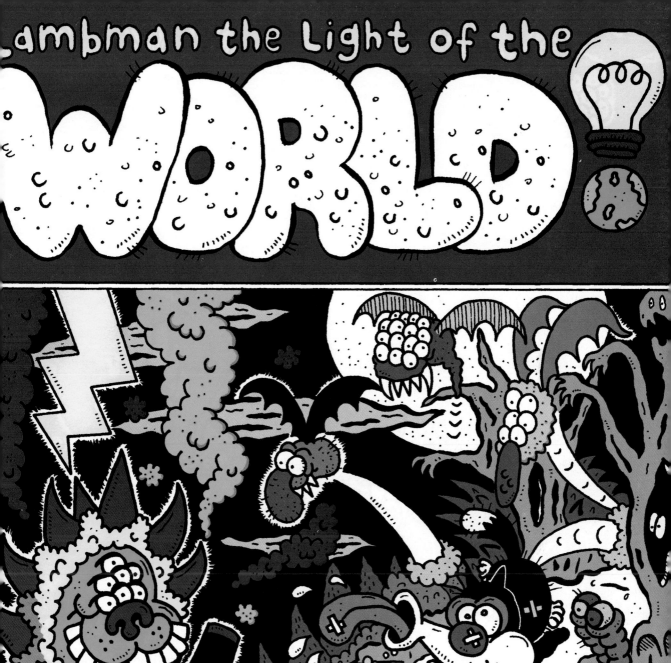

'I am the light of the world. Whoever follows me will never walk in darkness, but will have the light of life.' *John 8:12*

"THAT'S THE MOST AMAZING STORY I HAVE EVER READ," SAYS BASHO. HE FINDS THAT HE HAS A NEW RESPECT FOR THIS LAMBMAN. "YEAH, HE'S THE BEST OF THE BEST," WHISPERS SIR RAPH WHO BEAMS AT HIS MASTER AND FRIEND MURMURING JOYFULLY, "MOST BEST."

FOR THE FIRST TIME BASHO SEES HIS OWN FAVOURITE
BEAST FOR WHAT IT REALLY IS. HE SEES THE BEAST
BEHIND THE SHADOW IN ITS TRUE FORM...
...AND HE IS ASHAMED.

AND SO HE DOES. BASHO EATS THE BOOK, BITE BY BITE, RIGHT UP. IT TASTES LIKE...

CHOCOLATE

JELLY-BABIES

MARSHMALLO

ÉCLAIRS

COOKIES

JAM TARTS

BUTTERSCOTCH MILKSHAKE

...ALL OF BASHO'S FAVOURITE

AND AS HE WATCHES THE TRANSFORMATION, BASHO'S EYES CHANGE TOO — AND MANY THINGS ELSE BESIDES. THE BOOK IS WORKING FROM HIS INSIDES OUT!

FROM HERE ON LAMBMAN IS BASHO'S BEST FRIEN
TOGETHER. "FOLLOW ME!" CRIES LAMBMAN. "WE'LL GO
COLLECT SOME FRIENDS OF MINE!"

HEY DREAM OF ALL THE ADVENTURES THEY WILL HAVE
ACK TO YOUR BIRTHDAY BONANZA, BUT ON THE WAY LET'S

HAT'S UP BEHEMOTH? COMING TO MY NEW
RIEND'S PARTY!?"

BASHO WONDERS HOW THE PARTY IS GOING
WITHOUT HIM. "HOW WILL WE GET BACK IN TIME,
LAMBMAN?" HE ASKS. "NO WORRIES," SAID LAMBMAN
WITH A DOUBLE CLASH OF HIS HOOVES.

"WHO ARE YOUR NEW FRIENDS, BASHO? THEIR COSTUMES ARE AWESOME!" BASHO IS SAD ABOUT HIS TOY BUT HE FORGIVES THEM AND INVITES THEM TO PLAY A NEW GAME WITH LAMBMAN AND THE OTHERS.

LAMBMAN LOOKS TOTALLY DIFFERENT NOW. HE ANNOUNCES, "TODAY IS BASHO'S RE-BIRTHDAY!" BASHO THINKS IT IS THE MOST AWESOME BIRTHDAY EVER AS HE DIGS INTO AN AMPLE-SIZED HELPING OF TRIPLE-CHOCOLATE-FUDGE-CHUNK-BIRTHDAY-CAKE!

WELL, IT COULD HAPPEN TO ANYONE (EVEN YOU). EVERY BOY AND GIRL SHOULD...BEWARE OF THE BIBLICAL BEASTIES!

THE 10-HORNED 7-HEADED BEAST FROM THE SEA

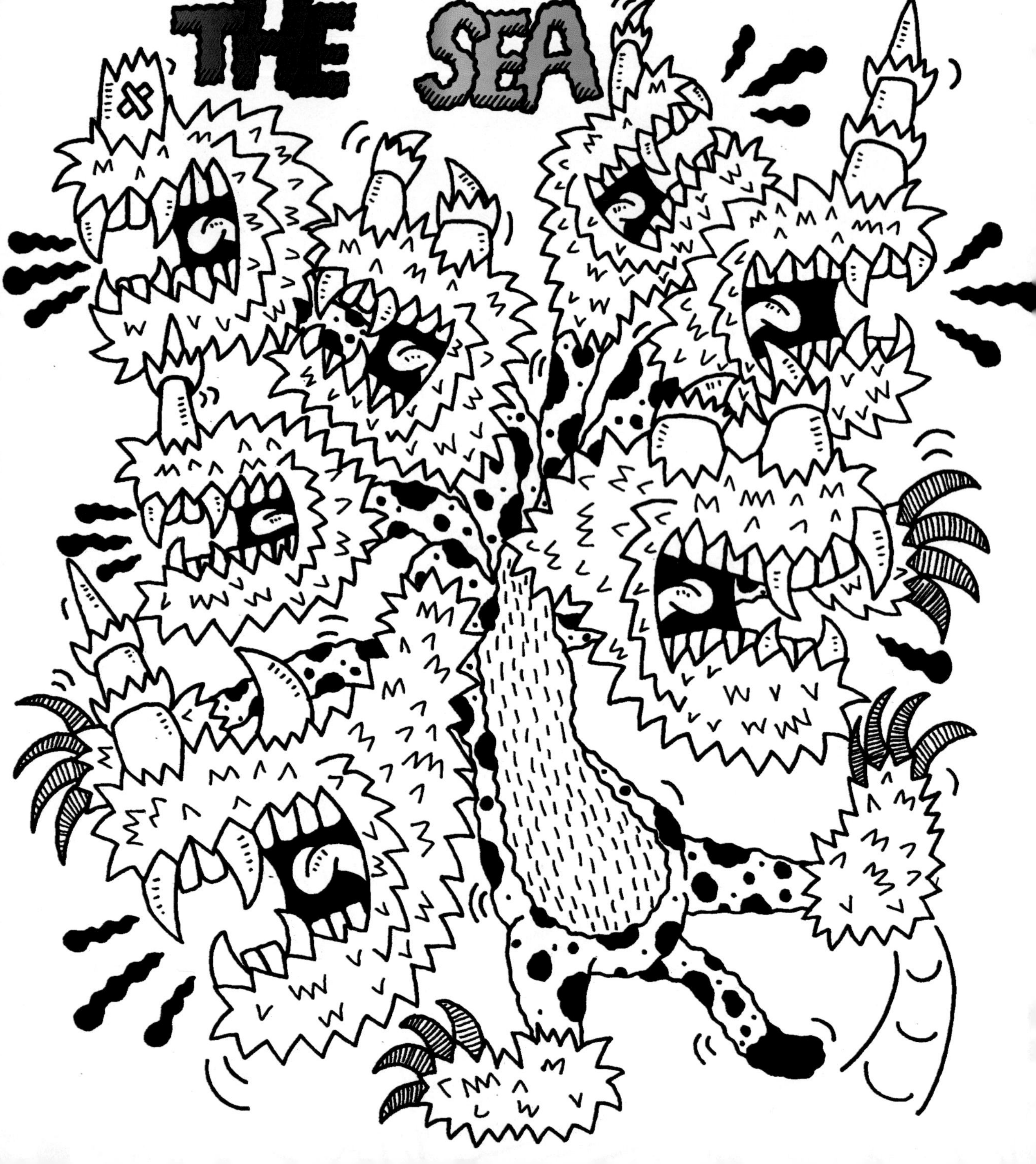

THE OLD SERPENT